MACMILL

PRE-INTERN

GW00399930

IAN FLEMING

Casino Royale

Retold by John Escott

PRE-INTERMEDIATE LEVEL

Founding Editor: John Milne

The Macmillan Readers provide a choice of enjoyable reading materials for learners of English. The series is published at six levels – Starter, Beginner, Elementary, Pre-intermediate, Intermediate and Upper.

Level control

Information, structure and vocabulary are controlled to suit the students' ability at each level.

The number of words at each level:

Starter	about 300 basic words
Beginner	about 600 basic words
Elementary	about 1100 basic words
Pre-intermediate	about 1400 basic words
Intermediate	about 1600 basic words
Upper	about 2200 basic words

Vocabulary

Some difficult words and phrases in this book are important for understanding the story. Some of these words are explained in the story and some are shown in the pictures. From Pre-intermediate level upwards, words are marked with a number like this: ...³. These words are explained in the Glossary at the end of the book.

Answer keys

Answer keys for the *Points for Understanding* and the *Exercises* sections can be found at www.macmillanenglish.com

Contents

A Note About The Author

Ian Lancaster Fleming was born on the 28th of May 1908 in Canterbury, England. He was a newspaper journalist and a writer. He created one of the most famous characters in twentieth-century fiction – James Bond.

Ian Fleming was educated at Eton – a famous school for boys. After he left Eton, he trained to be a soldier at Sandhurst Military Academy. He then went to Europe to study languages at Munich and Geneva universities.

Fleming's first job was as a journalist. From 1929 to 1933, he worked in Moscow for a news agency called *Reuters*. In this job, Fleming heard about Soviet spies who sold government secrets to other countries. Fleming sent reports about these spies to Reuters in London. He returned to London in 1933.

In the Second World War (1939–1945), Fleming was an officer at the headquarters of the British Navy. Here, he learnt a lot about spying and how to collect secret information – intelligence. After the war, he worked for the *Sunday Times* newspaper.

Fleming decided to become a writer during the war. He wrote about spies and dangerous criminals. In 1952, he finished his first novel. In the same year, he married Anne Rothermere. He was 44 years old.

Fleming's first novel – *Casino Royale* – was about a handsome British secret agent called James Bond. Bond was a spy who loved women, fast cars, and good food and drink. He was well-paid because his job was very dangerous. James Bond also had a 'Licence to Kill'. This meant that sometimes he was told to kill his enemies.

Casino Royale was very successful and the adventures of James Bond, agent number 007, became very popular. When

Fleming died on the 12th of August, 1964, more than 40 million copies of the James Bond books had been sold. The books are: *Casino Royale* (1953), *Live and Let Die* (1954), *Moonraker* (1955), *Diamonds Are Forever* (1956), *From Russia With Love* (1957), *Doctor No* (1958), *Goldfinger* (1959), *For Your Eyes Only* (1960), *Thunderball* (1961), *The Spy Who Loved Me* (1962), *On Her Majesty's Secret Service* (1963), *You Only Live Twice* (1964), *The Man With the Golden Gun* (1965) and *Octopussy* and *The Living Daylights* (1966).

The story of *Dr No* was made into a film in 1962. The film starred the actor Sean Connery, and the Bond films continue to be huge international successes. By 2006, five actors had starred as James Bond. Millions of people all over the world have seen and loved the films.

A Note About This Story

The story of *Casino Royale* takes place in the 1950s. The names of some countries and their governments have changed since that time.

In October 1917, a communist government came into power in Russia. The communists believed that everyone had to share everything – money, power and land. Russia joined together with the other countries which it controlled. This group of countries was called the Union of Soviet Socialist Republics (the USSR) and Moscow became its capital.

From 1928, Joseph Stalin led the Soviet Union. He ruled over the Russian people for more than 25 years. Stalin created a special government department, the MGB. The MGB made sure that the country and its people were safe. This department later became the secret police force called the KGB. Officers of the KGB collected information about the USSR's enemies. The KGB tried to protect the country and its people. Sometimes the KGB secretly investigated the people of the USSR. SMERSH was part of the KGB. The letters S-M-E-R-S-H are from the Russian words 'Smyert Shpionam' which mean, 'Death to Spies'. People were very afraid of SMERSH.

During the Second World War, France, Britain, the United States and the Soviet Union fought together – they were allies. But when the war ended in May 1945, these countries began to disagree with each other. France, Britain and the United States believed that democratic capitalism was the best political system. The USSR believed that communism was the better way.

Then other nations which believed in democracy became friends with the United States and Western Europe. And nations which believed in communism became allies with the Soviet Union.

The US and the USSR started to build huge numbers of powerful weapons, including atomic bombs – powerful bombs which could destroy whole cities. Each country watched the other. They did not trust each other and they made life difficult for each other. This period – 1945 to 1989 – was called the Cold War.

During the Cold War, many countries had secret intelligence services. These services sent men and women into their enemies' countries. These spies tried to discover their enemies' secrets. They also tried to find their enemies' spies. Sometimes they tried to kill them.

In 1991, the communists lost power in the USSR. Soon the Soviet Union broke up. By the end of 1993, the independent republics of Armenia, Azerbaijan, Belarus, Georgia, Kazakhstan, Kyrgyzstan, Moldova, Russia, Tajikistan, Turkmenistan, Ukraine and Uzbekistan were all members of the CIS (The Commonwealth of Independent States). Russia's neighbours around the Baltic Sea – Lithuania, Latvia and Estonia – were independent countries.

Ian Fleming's James Bond stories are set during the Cold War. It was a dangerous time and many people were frightened of an atomic war. So they loved to read about James Bond's exciting adventures with powerful enemies, fast cars and beautiful women.

The People in This Story

James Bond

M

Vesper Lynd

Le Chiffre

Rene Mathis

Felix Leiter

Gunman 1

Gunman 2

'Black Patch'

1

A Memorandum[1] *for* M

The memorandum came to M from the Head of Station S of the Secret Service. It read:

SUBJECT:

LE CHIFFRE, RUSSIA'S CHIEF AGENT IN FRANCE –
A PLAN FOR HIS DESTRUCTION.

THIS INFORMATION WAS GIVEN TO US BY ONE OF LE CHIFFRE'S GIRLFRIENDS.

LE CHIFFRE IS TREASURER[2] OF **SODA**. SODA IS A COMMUNIST-CONTROLLED TRADE UNION[3] IN FRANCE.

LE CHIFFRE IS NEAR FINANCIAL RUIN[4]. IN JANUARY 1946, HE 'BORROWED' FIFTY MILLION FRANCS[5] FROM SODA'S FUNDS. HE USED THE MONEY TO MAKE BAD INVESTMENTS[6]. THESE INVESTMENTS ARE NOW WORTH NOTHING.

LE CHIFFRE HOPES TO REPAY THE MONEY TO SODA. HE HAS RENTED A SMALL VILLA NEAR ROYALE-LES-EAUX FOR A WEEK FROM 15 JUNE. LE CHIFFRE WILL TRY TO WIN FIFTY MILLION FRANCS PLAYING BACCARAT[7].

THIS POWERFUL RUSSIAN AGENT MUST BE DESTROYED. THIS WILL HAPPEN IF LE CHIFFRE DOES NOT WIN AT ROYALE.

WE MUST SEND OUR BEST GAMBLER[8] **TO ROYALE. OUR MAN MUST BEAT LE CHIFFRE AT BACCARAT.**

NOTE A) LE CHIFFRE IS ABOUT 45 YEARS OLD. HEIGHT 1.70M. WEIGHT 114.3KG. HAIR RED-BROWN. EYES DARK BROWN. HE SPEAKS FRENCH, GERMAN, ENGLISH

Bond was stopped by M's cold eyes.
'Le Chiffre can have bad luck, too,' M replied.

AND RUSSIAN. HE DRIVES FAST CARS AND IS A GOOD
GAMBLER. HE ALWAYS TRAVELS WITH TWO ARMED
GUARDS. HE IS A CLEVER AND DANGEROUS RUSSIAN
AGENT.

NOTE B) SMERSH IS THE MOST POWERFUL AND FEARED
ORGANIZATION IN RUSSIA. SMERSH'S JOB IS TO FIND
AND KILL ALL ENEMIES OF THE RUSSIAN SECRET
SERVICE AND SECRET POLICE. WE NEED TO LEARN
MORE ABOUT THIS ORGANIZATION. WE NEED TO
DESTROY ITS AGENTS.

Commander James Bond was an agent of the British Secret
Service. He was a handsome man with blue eyes and dark
hair. His interview with M was short.

'Well, Bond?' asked M, when Bond had finished reading
the memorandum.

Bond looked across the desk at M.

'I'd like to do it,' he said. 'But I can't promise I'll win. I
could have bad luck and – .'

Bond was stopped by M's cold eyes. Of course M knew
this. M was Head of the British Secret Service. It was M's job
to know Bond's chances of winning at baccarat.

'Le Chiffre can have bad luck, too,' M replied. 'You'll
have twenty-five million francs. We will give you ten million
now. Then we will send you another ten million later.' He
smiled. 'You can win the extra five million yourself. I'll ask
headquarters at Deuxieme to send Mathis. You did a good job
with him at the Casino in Monte Carlo. I'll also tell the
CIA[9] in Washington to send somebody. Make sure that you
win. And be careful. Le Chiffre is a dangerous man. Good
luck.'

'Thank you, sir,' said Bond. He went to the door.

'Wait a minute,' said M. 'I may send you an assistant.

They can contact you at Royale. Don't worry, it will be someone good.'

Bond liked to work alone, but he didn't argue with M.

'Yes, sir,' he said, and left the room.

2

Mathis and the Microphone[10]

Two weeks later, James Bond was sitting in the Casino at Royale-les-Eaux. It was three in the morning and the air was filled with cigarette smoke. Le Chiffre was still playing – and still winning. Bond watched him for some minutes. Then he collected his winnings[11] from the cashier[12] and left the Casino. He walked across the road and through the gardens of the Hotel Splendide.

The *concierge*[13] gave him his key for room 45 and a cable[14]. The cable was from Jamaica. It read:

KINGSTON JAMAICA

BOND SPLENDIDE ROYALE-LES-EAUX

HAVANA CIGAR CUBAN FACTORIES PRODUCTION

THE NUMBER YOU NEED IS TEN MILLION

Earlier that afternoon, Bond had asked his headquarters in London for more money. The cable was a sort of code[15]. It meant that his headquarters were sending him ten million francs.

Bond was pretending to be the son of a Jamaican millionaire. That was his 'cover'[16].

He wrote a reply to the cable:

THANKS. INFORMATION SHOULD BE ENOUGH – BOND

Bond gave the reply to the *concierge* and said goodnight. Then he walked upstairs to the door of his room. He took out a gun from under his jacket. Then he opened the door quickly and switched on the light. There was nobody in the room but Bond did not feel stupid. He had to be very careful in his job.

13

Bond undressed and had a cold shower. Then he lit a cigarette. He had arrived at Royale-les-Eaux two days before. The last two afternoons and nights he had played roulette at the Casino. He had watched Le Chiffre at the tables. The Russian was a clever and lucky gambler.

So far, Bond had won three million francs. He had started with ten million. Now London was sending him another ten. So he had twenty-three million francs to gamble with. Bond put the money under his pillow and climbed into bed.

For ten minutes, he thought about everything that had happened that day. Then he slept.

The next morning Bond had a cold shower. Then he ate his breakfast at a table in front of the window. He was looking at the sea when the telephone rang. It was the *concierge*.

'A man from Radio Stentor is here with the radio that you ordered, monsieur[17],' the *concierge* said.

'Send him up,' said Bond.

When Mathis came in, Bond smiled.

'I've just arrived from Paris, monsieur,' said Mathis. 'Here is the radio.' He put the radio on the floor and switched it on. The sound of loud music filled the room. Mathis walked across to Bond and shook his hand.

Bond smiled. 'Now, why – ?' he began.

'My dear friend,' said Mathis. 'Your cover has been spoilt! The Russians know who you are.'

Mathis looked up at the ceiling. Then he pointed to the chimney[18].

'A few centimetres up the chimney is a radio microphone,' he explained. 'Its wires go up to the room above. They can hear everything.' Then Mathis smiled. 'Now for some more play-acting,' he said. He walked over to the radio and switched it off.

'Are you happy, monsieur?' he asked.

'Very happy,' said Bond. 'The music is beautiful. Let's hear the rest of it.'

Mathis grinned and switched the radio on again. 'Now to business,' he said. 'You will be pleased with your assistant – your Number Two. She is very beautiful, and she is also a radio expert. We will pretend that she works with me. We're both staying in the hotel. So my "assistant" will be near you.' He smiled. 'Day . . . or night.'

But Bond did not smile back at him.

'Why did they send me a woman?' he said, angrily. 'This isn't a game!'

'Relax, James,' said Mathis. 'She's good at her job and she speaks French very well. She will meet you at the Casino. You are the rich son of a millionaire. It's normal for you to find a pretty girl to . . . uh . . . share your winnings with.'

'Are there any other surprises?' asked Bond.

'Not really,' replied Mathis. 'Le Chiffre's villa is about sixteen kilometres down the coast road. He has got two guards with him. They speak to each other in Bulgarian.'

'Anything else?' asked Bond.

'Come to the Hermitage Bar before lunch,' said Mathis. 'And meet your Number Two. Ask her to dinner, then she can come to the Casino with you tonight. I'll be there, but you probably won't see me. Oh, and there's an American called Felix Leiter. He's staying here. He's the CIA man.'

After Mathis left, Bond sat back at the window. He was not happy. The Russians knew that he was here. They might try to kill him.

And then there was the problem of the girl. Bond did not like working with women.

3

The Girl from London

It was twelve o'clock when Bond left the hotel. He decided to drive down the coast road. He wanted to look at Le Chiffre's villa.

An hour later, Bond walked into the Hermitage Bar. He went to a table near one of the windows. He ordered a drink and looked round at the expensively-dressed customers.

After some minutes, he saw Mathis on the pavement outside. He was with a dark-haired girl. Bond waited for them to come into the bar. He pretended not to see them.

'It's Monsieur Bond!' said Mathis. 'Are you waiting for someone? No? This is my assistant, Mademoiselle Lynd. My dear, this gentleman is from Jamaica. I took a radio to his hotel this morning.'

'Would you both like to have a drink with me?' asked Bond. He called the waiter and ordered drinks. Then the two men talked about the weather and about Royale-les-Eaux.

The girl sat silently. Her hair was very black, her eyes were deep blue. Bond was excited by her beauty. But the girl seemed cool and uninterested.

After some time, Mathis turned to her.

'Excuse me,' he said, 'but I must telephone the Dubernes about dinner tonight. Do you mind eating alone this evening?'

'No,' she answered. 'It's all right.'

Mathis went to the telephone near the bar. Bond looked at the girl.

'It's not good to eat alone,' he said to her. 'Would you like to have dinner with me tonight?'

'This is my assistant, Mademoiselle Lynd.'

'I'd like that very much,' she said warmly. She smiled. 'And then we could go to the Casino. Perhaps I'll bring you good luck.'

They arranged a time and a place to meet. Bond felt that she was excited about the job. Perhaps they could work well together. She was beautiful, and he wanted to sleep with her. But only when the job was finished.

Mathis came back to the table and Bond called to the waiter for his bill.

'I have to get back to the hotel,' he said.

Mathis and the girl watched him leave. Then Mathis moved closer to her.

'James is my very good friend,' he said. 'I'm glad that you've met each other.'

'He's very good-looking,' the girl replied after a moment. 'But there's something cold and – '

Suddenly, there was an explosion[19] outside the bar. The window behind them shattered[20]. Mathis and the girl were pushed back into their chairs. There were screams, and people began to run towards the door.

'Stay here,' Mathis said to the girl.

Then he jumped out of his chair and climbed through the broken window.

4

The Men in Dark Suits

After Bond left the bar, he walked towards his hotel. The day was beautiful and the sun was very hot. As he walked, Bond noticed two men on the opposite side of the road. They were standing quietly under a tree, about a hundred metres away.

There was something strange about the two men. They were both small, and they both wore dark suits. Each man had a square camera case. One case was red, the other case was blue.

When Bond was fifty metres away, Red-man looked at Blue-man. Then Blue-man did something with his case. Bond could not see what he was doing because there was a tree in front of him. Suddenly, there was a flash of white light and an explosion.

The explosion threw Bond down onto the pavement. Then pieces of clothes began to fall around him. The clothes were covered in blood. Black smoke filled the sky.

There was nothing left of the two men in dark suits.

―――

When Mathis got to Bond, he was leaning against the tree that had saved his life.

Ambulances and fire engines began to arrive. Mathis helped Bond back to the Hotel Splendide.

In Bond's room, Mathis asked questions while Bond took off his blood-spotted clothes. When Bond told him about the two men, Mathis picked up the telephone.

'. . . tell the police that Bond's not hurt,' Mathis said quickly to the person on the other end of the telephone line. 'I'll explain everything to them. Tell the newspapers that it was a fight between two Bulgarians. One killed the other with a bomb. There was probably a third Bulgarian watching. Say nothing about him. He'll try to get away. The police must catch him.'

Mathis put down the phone and turned to Bond. 'You were lucky,' he said. 'They wanted that bomb to kill you. But something went wrong.' He smiled at Bond. 'Get a drink and some lunch, then have a rest.'

―――

Several hours later, Bond was drinking a whisky when the telephone rang.

'This is Mademoiselle Lynd,' said the voice, quietly. 'Are you all right?'

'Yes, thank you,' replied Bond.

'Good,' she said. 'Please take care of yourself.'

5

Felix Leiter

That evening, Bond walked across to the Casino. He had always been a gambler. He liked the luxury of the card-rooms and casinos. Sometimes he was lucky, sometimes not. But Bond believed that luck should be loved and not feared.

Bond changed a million francs into plaques and took a seat at Roulette Table Number 1. He played seventeen games. He lost some games and won some games. He finished with winnings of one million francs.

An American was sitting opposite. When Bond got up from the table, the American got up too.

'Let me buy you a drink,' the man said to Bond.

Bond guessed that the American was from the CIA. M had told him that they would send someone.

'My name's Felix Leiter,' said the American, as they walked to the bar.

'Mine is Bond – James Bond.'

They ordered drinks.

'A dry martini,' said Bond to the barman. 'But I want it in a large glass.'

'I'm pleased to be working with you,' Leiter said. He lit a cigarette. 'Our people in Washington are very interested in this job.'

'Our enemies already know about me,' said Bond. 'They probably know about you and Mathis, too. Please be at the Casino this evening. I've got an assistant, Miss Lynd. I'd like her to be with you when I start playing.' He smiled at Leiter. 'Be careful of Le Chiffre's two gunmen. They probably won't make any trouble. But we can't be sure.'

Felix Leiter was about thirty-five. He was tall and thin,

with fair hair. Leiter moved and spoke slowly. But Bond knew that he would be a good fighter.

Bond told him about his trip down the coast that morning. Leiter drank his second glass of whisky and listened carefully. Then, at seven-thirty, they walked back to the hotel together.

Leiter's room was on a higher floor than Bond's room. The two men arranged to see each other later, at the Casino.

Bond had a long, hot bath followed by an ice-cold shower. He lay down on his bed and thought about his plans for Mathis, Leiter and the girl. Then he thought about Le Chiffre and his other enemies.

At twenty minutes to nine, he dressed in trousers and a silk shirt. Next, he opened a drawer. He took out a light leather holster[21] and put it over his shoulder. Then he took a gun from the drawer. He dropped the gun into the holster and put his dinner jacket on. The gun was hidden under the jacket.

He felt cool and comfortable as he walked out of his room and locked the door. When he arrived in the hotel lobby, he heard a voice call,

'Good evening.'

The girl stepped out of the lift and waited for Bond. Her black velvet dress was simple but expensive. A thin diamond necklace hung around her throat. She carried a black evening bag.

Bond thought that she looked beautiful.

The girl held his arm as they went in to dinner. People in the crowded restaurant turned to look at her. Bond watched them and smiled. They went to a table in a quiet corner of the room.

'Would you like a drink?' asked Bond.

'I would love a glass of vodka,' she said.

Bond ordered two very cold vodkas.

'I don't know your first name,' he said to the girl.

'Vesper,' she said.

'Vesper?'

'It's an old word for "evening",' she explained. 'And I was born in the evening. Some people like it, others don't.'

'I think it's a fine name,' said Bond.

They ordered dinner and a bottle of champagne. The vodkas arrived and Bond held up his glass.

'Here's to luck, Vesper,' he said.

'Yes,' replied the girl, quietly. She held up her glass and looked into his eyes. Then she moved nearer to him.

'I have some news from Mathis,' she said. 'It's about the bomb. It's a fantastic story.'

Bond stared at her. 'Tell me,' he said.

'They found the third Bulgarian,' Vesper explained. 'He was on the road to Paris. Two policemen stopped him and asked for his papers. The three Bulgarians were part of a group here in France. These three men were going to get two million francs for killing you.'

She drank some of her vodka.

'An agent gave them the two camera cases,' she went on. '"The blue case contains a smoke bomb," he told them. "The red case is the explosive. When one of you throws the red case, the other must press a switch on the blue case. Then you can escape in the smoke from the smoke bomb." But he was lying. Both cases contained explosives. The plan was to kill you *and* the bombers at the same time. There was probably another plan to kill the third man.'

'Very clever,' said Bond. 'Go on.'

'The Bulgarians switched on the smoke bomb *first*,' she continued. 'Then they planned to throw the explosive bomb at you.'

'But they blew themselves up,' said Bond.

'Yes,' said Vesper. 'The third Bulgarian was waiting behind the Hotel Splendide. The police showed him bits of the red bomb. Then he knew that the agent had tricked the three of them. He started talking after that. But he knows nothing about Le Chiffre.'

The waiter arrived with the food. They ate in silence for some minutes. Then Bond drank some of his champagne and looked at her.

'What section are you in?' he asked.

'I'm personal assistant to Head of Section S,' said Vesper.

24

'Head of S asked M if I could come here. M said yes, but he said that you don't like working with women.'

When Bond said nothing, she went on, 'You're one of our heroes. A Double O agent.'

'It's not difficult to get a Double O number,' Bond said. 'If you're happy to kill people. Do you like the food?'

'It's lovely,' she said, smiling. 'I'm enjoying myself and – '

But she was stopped by the cold look in Bond's eyes.

'We're here to do a job,' he said. 'Remember that.'

Then Bond told her his plans. As she listened, Vesper remembered her boss's warning.

'Bond's a good-looking man,' Head of S had told her. 'But don't fall in love with him. He's got a cold heart. Good luck, and don't get hurt.'

Now, Bond was explaining the game of baccarat.

'Tonight Le Chiffre will be the banker,' Bond said. 'He has twenty-four million francs, and I've got about the same. There will be ten players, and a croupier who will collect the cards. I'll sit opposite Le Chiffre at the table.'

He drank some more champagne.

'The banker begins with a bet of five hundred thousand francs,' he went on. 'The person in the Number One chair can accept the bet. If he says no, then Number Two can bet. If Number Two doesn't want to bet, then it goes to Number Three, and on round the table. I'll try to accept the bet until either Le Chiffre or I have no money left. In the end, one of us must win.

'It's a simple game. I get two cards and the banker gets two. To win, I must have two or three cards which add up to nine, or the nearest number to nine. If one of us doesn't win immediately, we can take one more card. Picture cards and tens are worth nothing. Aces are worth one. Do you understand?'

'Yes,' said Vesper.

'The banker gives me two cards. If the two cards don't add up to nine, then I can ask for another card. I'll ask for the extra card if my cards add up to less than five. If they total six or seven, I may not ask for another card.

'The banker can look at his cards after I've asked for a card – or decided to "stand". If the banker's cards total nine, he wins. If they don't add up to nine, then he can choose another card.'

'I understand,' said Vesper.

'Good,' said Bond.

Some minutes later, he paid the bill and they left the restaurant.

It was time to gamble.

6

The Casino

In the main room of the Casino, Felix Leiter saw Bond and came to meet him.

'This is Vesper Lynd,' Bond told him.

'Perhaps I can show Miss Lynd how to play roulette, James,' said Leiter. 'Then we can come and watch you later.'

'I'd like that,' said Vesper.

'I'll leave you with my friend, Felix,' Bond said to Vesper. He smiled and walked away.

Bond collected his twenty-four million francs from the cashier. Then he walked across the room to the baccarat table. He sat down in chair Number Six and lit a cigarette.

The banker's chair opposite him was empty. Bond looked around the table. He knew most of the players. In chair Number Seven, on his right, sat Monsieur Sixte, a rich Belgian. In Number Nine was Lord Danvers, a weak-looking man with a rich American wife. She sat in chair Number Three. At Number One, on the right of the bank, was a famous Greek gambler. Bond knew that the Greek would play coldly and well.

At that moment, Le Chiffre arrived. He had a large white face, wide shoulders and reddish-brown hair. He smiled coldly at the players around the table. Then he sat down opposite Bond.

The game started. Le Chiffre was the banker. He took a card from the shoe and pushed it towards chair Number One. Then he took a card for himself. Then another for the Greek, and one more for himself. The croupier lifted the Greek's cards and dropped them next to the Greek's hands.

The Greek picked up the cards. He looked carefully at

them. Then he put them face-down on the table and looked at Le Chiffre.

'No,' said the Greek. He had not asked for another card.

Le Chiffre picked up his cards and turned them over. They were a four and a five. A nine.

The croupier turned over the Greek's cards. He had a seven and a queen. Le Chiffre had won.

'Seven,' the croupier said. He removed the cards.

Bond lit a cigarette and watched the Greek make another bet. The bank won again.

'A bank of two million francs,' said the croupier.

For a moment, nobody spoke. Two million was a very large bet.

Then Bond said, '*Banco*.' He was ready to play.

7

The Game

Le Chiffre and Bond looked at each other coolly. Then Bond put a packet of French francs on the table.

The other players watched. They could feel the coldness between the two gamblers. No one spoke as Le Chiffre took the four cards.

The croupier pushed Bond's two cards towards him. Bond looked at the cards quickly. Then he looked at Le Chiffre. After a moment, Bond turned his cards over.

They were a four and a five – a nine.

There was a little cry of surprise from the other players. Then Le Chiffre carelessly turned over his two cards. They were two picture cards – worth nothing.

The game went on. Bond looked at the people who were standing around the table. He soon saw Le Chiffre's two gunmen. They were standing behind the banker. The man by Le Chiffre's right arm was tall, with a grey face. The other man was short and dark. He had a flat head and a thick moustache. There was a wooden walking stick[22] next to him.

It was one o'clock in the morning and Bond had won four million francs. He now had twenty-eight million francs. Le Chiffre continued to play calmly.

The Greek at Number One was having a bad time. He lost a bet of half a million francs, and then another. He passed[23] on the third bet.

'A bank of two million,' said the croupier.

Players two and three passed.

'*Banco*,' said Monsieur Sixte – and lost the bet.

'A bank of four million francs,' said the croupier.

'*Banco*,' said Bond. The croupier pushed two new cards

towards him. Bond looked at them quickly. He had a dangerous total of five, but he did not take another card.

Le Chiffre turned over his two cards. He had a picture card and a four. He took another card from the shoe. It was a three.

'The bank has seven,' said the croupier. He turned over Bond's losing cards. 'Five,' he said. He took four million francs from Bond's money.

'A bank of eight million,' said the croupier.

Bond took the bet and lost again to Le Chiffre's nine. In two bets, he had lost twelve million francs. He had sixteen million francs left.

He looked across at Le Chiffre. 'Do you want to lose even more, Mr Bond?' the Russian's eyes seemed to ask.

Bond took some francs and plaques from his pocket. He pushed them into the centre of the table. His mouth had suddenly gone dry. Vesper and Felix Leiter had come to the table. Leiter looked worried, but Vesper smiled at him. The gunman with the stick was now behind Bond.

The croupier pushed Bond's two cards towards him. Bond looked at them. Then he looked again. He had an ace and a picture card.

'A card,' he said. He tried to sound calm.

Le Chiffre turned over his two cards. He had a picture card and a five. He took another card from the shoe. The croupier pushed it to Bond. It was a five.

Bond now had six and Le Chiffre had five. The banker took another card and turned it over. Le Chiffre needed a one, two, three or four to win.

It was a four. Le Chiffre had won.

Bond had lost all his money.

8

The Man with the Stick

Bond lit a cigarette. What next? Go back to the hotel. Make a phone call to London, then fly home. He would get a taxi to the offices in Regent's Park, then walk up the stairs to M's room. He would look into M's cold face across the desk.

'Better luck next time,' M would say.

But there couldn't be a 'next time'. This had been their best chance to destroy Le Chiffre. And Bond had lost.

He looked at the people around the table. The croupier counted the money and put the plaques in front of the banker. Would anyone bet against a bank of thirty-two million francs?

Leiter was not with Vesper now. Vesper looked strangely calm. She smiled at Bond.

'She doesn't understand the game,' Bond thought.

A waiter stopped beside him. He put a thick envelope on the table next to Bond. Bond's heart began to beat fast. He moved the envelope under the table and opened it. His hands were shaking, but he could feel the money inside. Excitement rushed through him. He slipped the francs into his pockets. There was a piece of paper with the money. It had one line of writing.

THIRTY-TWO MILLION FRANCS. WITH BEST WISHES FROM THE USA.

Bond looked towards Vesper. Felix Leiter was standing next to her again. Leiter smiled, and Bond smiled back.

This time Bond had to win. Or had Le Chiffre already got the fifty million francs that he needed to repay SODA? Perhaps he had. Then Le Chiffre wouldn't need to play.

The croupier had changed Bond's notes into plaques. They were in the middle of the table with the other plaques. Thirty-two million francs.

Le Chiffre did not move.

'A bank of thirty-two million,' said the croupier.

The players were silent.

'Maybe he needs to win one more bet,' thought Bond. 'I've got to accept the bet. It will surprise him. He won't expect anyone to take the whole thirty-two million bet.'

Bond was right. Le Chiffre needed another eight million francs. At last, the banker nodded to the croupier.

'A bank of thirty-two million francs,' the croupier said.

'*Banco*,' Bond said quietly.

He pushed the money across the table. At that moment, he saw Le Chiffre look at the gunman behind him.

Immediately, Bond felt something hard against his back.

'This is a gun, monsieur,' a voice whispered. 'It's silent. It can blow a hole in your back but it will make no sound. People will think that you've fainted[24]. Now, take back your bet before I count to ten. If you call for help, I'll shoot you.'

Now Bond understood. The 'walking stick' was really a gun.

'One,' said the voice.

Bond turned his head. The man was smiling at him.

'Two.'

Suddenly, Bond pushed himself backwards as hard as he could. He moved so fast that the chair knocked the 'walking stick' from the gunman's hand. The chair broke into two pieces. People crowded around him.

'Monsieur! Are you all right?' someone asked.

'Shall we get a doctor?' another person said.

Two or three people helped Bond to stand up.

'Thank you,' Bond said. 'I'm all right now. It was only a moment's faintness. I was a little hot.'

Bond moved so fast that the chair knocked the 'stick' from the gunman's hand.

Someone brought a new chair and Bond sat down. He looked across at Le Chiffre. He could see fear in the banker's fat, white face. He turned to look at the people behind him. The gunman had gone. A waiter was holding the stick.

Bond called and the waiter came across to him. 'Please give that "walking stick" to that gentleman,' said Bond. He pointed at Felix Leiter. 'It belongs to a friend of his.'

When Leiter looked closely at the walking stick, he would understand why Bond had 'fainted'. Bond turned back to the table. He was ready.

9

Winner and Loser

It was two o'clock in the morning. This time Bond must not lose.

Two cards were pushed towards him. Le Chiffre watched him from the other side of the table. Bond took the cards and looked at them.

He had two picture cards. They were worth nothing.

'A card,' said Bond.

Le Chiffre turned over his own two cards. A picture card and a three.

'Three,' said the croupier.

Le Chiffre took a card and slowly turned it over. It was a nine. A lovely nine! The croupier pushed it to Bond.

Now it was Le Chiffre's turn to decide. He needed a six to make a total of nine. It was a difficult decision. He did not know what Bond's first two cards had been.

Le Chiffre looked at Bond's cards. Then he looked at his own cards. His face was hot.

Finally, Le Chiffre took his card and turned it over. It was a wonderful card – a five.

'The bank has eight,' said the croupier.

Bond sat silently. Le Chiffre smiled. Le Chiffre was sure that Bond's cards would add up to more than nine. Every person watching thought that Bond had lost.

The croupier turned over Bond's first two cards. They were picture cards and worth nothing.

'Nine,' said the croupier.

The people around the table shouted with surprise. Bond was watching Le Chiffre. The big man fell back in his chair. His mouth opened and shut, and his face was grey.

The croupier pushed the plaques across to Bond. Then Le Chiffre took a packet of notes from his pocket. He threw them on the table. The croupier counted them.

'A bank of ten million francs,' the croupier said.

'That's all his money,' thought Bond. 'And if he loses now, no one will give him any more.'

'*Banco*,' said Bond. He looked straight at Le Chiffre.

Once more, the croupier pushed two cards across to him. Bond looked at them and turned them over.

'Nine,' said the croupier.

Le Chiffre looked at his own two cards. They were picture cards.

The croupier pushed the plaques across to Bond.

Le Chiffre watched the plaques, then he stood up slowly. He pushed past the other players. People moved to let him go past. They looked at him strangely.

He was like a man who carried the smell of death. Then he was gone.

Bond stood up. He asked the croupier to take his winnings to the cashier. The other players were getting up from their chairs. There could not be a game without a banker.

Bond said goodnight to them. Then he went to meet Vesper and Felix Leiter. They walked across to the cashier.

Bond took Felix Leiter's money in notes, and took a cheque for the rest of his winnings. He walked over to the bar and gave Leiter his thirty-two million francs back. For a few minutes they drank champagne and talked about the game. Leiter took a bullet[25] from his pocket.

'It's from the walking stick-gun,' he said. 'I gave the gun to Mathis. The gunman escaped but they've got his fingerprints[26] from the gun. Perhaps we'll find out more about him in the morning.'

Bond touched his jacket pocket.

'I'll take my winnings to the hotel,' he said. He turned to

Le Chiffre was like a man who carried the smell of death.

Vesper. 'Would you like a glass of champagne in the nightclub? It's called the Roi Galant.'

'I'd like that,' said Vesper. 'I'll meet you in the lobby.'

'Will you come, too, Felix?' asked Bond. But he was hoping to be alone with Vesper.

'I would like to go to bed,' Leiter said. He knew what Bond was thinking. 'But I'll come to the hotel with you.'

At the hotel, Leiter walked with Bond up to his room.

'Will you and Vesper be OK?' asked Leiter. 'Or would you like me to stay with you?'

'Go and get some sleep,' said Bond. 'Don't worry, I'm going to hide the cheque. They won't be interested in me without the money. Thanks for all your help.'

Leiter smiled. Then he went out and closed the door.

Bond went to the bathroom and washed his face in cold water. Twice that day he had nearly died. Would Le Chiffre's men try to kill him again? Or was Le Chiffre already on a boat? Was he trying to escape from SMERSH?

Bond took the cheque from his pocket. Then he opened the door of his room. There was nobody outside. He began to work with a small screwdriver[27].

Five minutes later, Bond closed and locked the door. Then he went down the stairs.

10

Kidnapped

The entrance to the Roi Galant was in a corner of the roulette room. The night club was small and dark. A band – guitar, piano and drums – was playing in a corner. Bond and Vesper sat at a table near the door. Bond ordered a bottle of champagne and a breakfast of eggs and bacon.

They sat and listened to the music for a time. Then Bond turned and looked at Vesper.

'It's wonderful to be with you,' he said. 'The job is finished, and it's a lovely end to the day.'

He expected her to smile, but she didn't.

'Yes, it is,' she said. She looked nervous.

'Maybe it's because I was cool to her earlier this evening,' Bond thought.

He drank champagne and talked about the day. He spoke about Mathis and Leiter, Le Chiffre and SMERSH.

'I've telephoned Paris from the hotel,' Vesper said. 'I've left a message for M about the game.'

This was all she said. She drank her champagne and did not look at Bond. Bond was disappointed. He drank a lot of champagne and ordered another bottle. They ate their eggs and bacon silently.

At four o'clock, a waiter came to the table.

'I have a note for Miss Lynd,' he said.

He gave Vesper a piece of paper. She read the note quickly.

'It's from Mathis,' she told Bond. 'He wants me to meet him at the Casino entrance hall. He's got a message for you. He's probably not wearing evening clothes and he doesn't want to come in. I'll only be a minute or two. Then perhaps

39

we can go home.' She smiled quickly. 'I've not been very friendly tonight. I'm sorry. It's been a difficult day.'

'It's OK,' said Bond. 'I'll pay the bill.'

Bond watched her walk to the entrance, then he lit a cigarette. He was suddenly tired. He called for the bill and took a last drink of champagne.

As he drank, Bond wondered about the note to Vesper. It seemed strange. Why hadn't Mathis asked them both to come to the Casino entrance hall?

Something was wrong.

Bond paid the bill and walked quickly through the gaming room. He looked up and down the long entrance hall.

No Vesper. No Mathis.

He ran to the entrance. The night air was cold.

Suddenly, he heard a small cry and the sound of a car door closing. Then a Citroën raced out of the wide entrance gate. As he watched, Bond saw someone throw something small and black from one of the windows. It fell into the flowers by the gate. Then the Citroën raced towards the coast road.

Bond ran to the gate. He picked up Vesper's black evening bag from amongst the flowers. Inside was the note. It read:

Can you come to the entrance hall for a moment?

I have news for Bond.
Rene Mathis.

It was not Mathis's writing.
Bond ran to his car.

11

The Crash

Soon Bond was speeding along the coast road. There was no wind, and the night was clear.

Bond drove faster and faster. He was angry. Why had M sent Vesper – *a woman* – on this job? He knew that Le Chiffre's men would give him the girl if he gave them the cheque. Well, he wouldn't do it! This job was more important than Vesper. All right, he would try and catch the Citroën. But if he didn't catch them, he would go back to his hotel. He would say nothing to Mathis about the Citroën. He would not pay Le Chiffre's men the forty million francs. Tomorrow he would show Mathis the note. He would ask Mathis what had happened to Vesper.

Bond's Bentley[28] was travelling at 160 kilometres an hour. The Citroën was only a kilometre or two ahead.

Bond took a gun from under the driver's seat. He put it on the seat beside him.

There were three men and the girl in the Citroën. Le Chiffre was driving. The man who had carried the walking stick-gun was beside him. There was a thick handle[29] next to the man's left hand. The handle came from the floor of the car.

The tall, thin gunman was sitting in the back seat. Vesper was next to him. She had a sack[30] over her head. It was tied around her neck with a piece of rope.

Le Chiffre watched Bond's car in his driving mirror. The Bentley was only a kilometre behind. When he went round a corner, Le Chiffre slowed to fifty kilometres an hour. He could see a crossroads[31] ahead.

'Get ready,' he said to the man beside him.

The man put his fingers round the handle. At that moment, the Bentley's headlights came round the corner.

'Now!' said Le Chiffre.

The man pulled the handle up quickly. Suddenly, the boot[32] at the back of the car opened wide. There was the sound of metal hitting the road. Le Chiffre looked into the mirror. Bond's car was coming round the corner. Le Chiffre quickly drove the car into a side road. At the same time, he turned off the car's lights.

He stopped the car and all three men jumped out. They ran back to the crossroads. Each man carried a gun.

The Bentley was speeding towards them.

12

The Villa

Bond could not see the Citroën when he came round the corner. He saw the crossroads ahead and started to slow down. But he was too late. Suddenly there was a 'carpet' of metal spikes[33] under his wheels. They tore the Bentley's tyres.

Bond could not control the heavy car. It hit the wall at the side of the road and turned over. Bond was thrown onto the floor of the car. There was the sound of breaking glass and metal on concrete. Then the Bentley stopped moving.

Le Chiffre and his two gunmen ran towards the car.

'Put your guns away and get him out,' said Le Chiffre. 'Be careful, I don't want a dead man. And hurry!'

The two men pulled Bond from the car. He was not conscious[34].

'Tie his arms,' said Le Chiffre. 'Put him in the car. Take everything from his pockets and give me his gun.'

Le Chiffre took Bond's gun. Then he walked back to the Citroën.

Bond was conscious now. Every part of his body hurt, but there were no bones broken. The two gunmen pushed him into the back seat of the Citroën.

Bond felt sick and weak. No one knew where he was. No one would miss him until the morning. They would find the Bentley. But they would not know the car was Bond's until later.

Then there was Vesper. He looked past the thin man.

'Vesper,' he said quietly.

She did not answer. Bond was suddenly afraid that she was dead. But then she moved under the sack.

At the same time, the thin man hit Bond twice.

Suddenly there was a 'carpet' of metal spikes under Bond's wheels.

'Silence,' the man said.

Bond lay back against the seat with his eyes closed. He blamed himself for his situation. He hadn't been careful enough. Instead, he had sat in the Roi Galant drinking champagne with Vesper.

All this time, Le Chiffre had said nothing. The third man shut the boot of the car. The man got in and sat beside him.

The Citroën raced along the coast road. Bond guessed that it was about five o'clock in the morning. He also guessed that they were only two or three kilometres away from Le Chiffre's villa.

Bond knew why the men had taken Vesper. They had known that Bond would try to rescue her. For the first time since the car crash, he began to feel afraid.

Ten minutes later, the Citroën turned left into a small side road. It went through some open gates and stopped outside the front door of Le Chiffre's villa.

Le Chiffre opened the door of the house with a key. Then the thin man pushed Bond out of the car. Le Chiffre went inside the house and the thin man pushed Vesper in after him. Bond followed her. He heard the third gunman lock the door behind him.

Le Chiffre was standing near the open door of a room. He waved to Bond. He was telling Bond to come to the room. The third gunman was taking Vesper away to the back of the house.

Suddenly, Bond kicked the thin man hard on the legs. The man cried out in pain and Bond ran after Vesper. His hands were tied but his feet were free.

The third gunman heard Bond coming. The man turned quickly. Bond kicked him hard in the stomach, and the man fell back against the wall. Bond tried to kick him again but the gunman caught his shoe. He twisted Bond's foot and Bond crashed to the ground.

For a moment, Bond lay still. Then the thin man came and pulled him up against the wall. He had a gun in his hand. He used it to hit Bond hard across the legs. Bond cried out with pain and fell onto his knees.

A door banged shut. Vesper and the third gunman had disappeared. Bond turned his head to the right and saw Le Chiffre.

'Come here, my dear friend,' said Le Chiffre. He spoke calmly in English. 'Let's not waste any more time.'

Bond walked towards him. There was nothing more that he could do.

13

Torture[35]

They took Bond to a large room. There was a large wooden chair by the window. There was also a low table with a glass on it, and a smaller, lighter chair.

Le Chiffre pointed at the smaller chair.

'Use that chair,' he told the thin man. 'Get him ready.'

He turned to Bond. 'Take off your clothes,' he said. 'Do it, or we will break your fingers. We're serious people, Mr Bond. We don't care if you live or die.'

Le Chiffre nodded to the thin man. Then he turned and left the room.

The thin man took a knife from his pocket. He cut the rope round Bond's arms. Then he moved quickly away from Bond. A moment later, the thin man pulled Bond's jacket down his back. Bond could not move his arms.

The knife cut through the cloth. Suddenly Bond's arms were free. Then the two halves of his jacket fell in front of him.

'Now, take off the rest of your clothes,' the thin man said.

Bond slowly started to take off his shirt.

Le Chiffre came quietly into the room. He was carrying a pot of coffee in one hand, and a large stick in the other hand. Le Chiffre put the coffee on the small table near the window and sat in the wooden chair. He pulled the other chair across so that it was opposite him. Then he poured some coffee into the glass.

Bond stood naked[36] in the middle of the room.

'Sit down,' Le Chiffre said. He pointed to the small chair.

Bond sat down. The thin man tied his arms and legs to the chair. Bond could not move.

The gunman left the room and closed the door.

Le Chiffre lit a cigarette and drank some coffee. He stared into Bond's eyes. Then he hit Bond hard in the stomach with the stick.

Bond could not breathe for several seconds. He closed his eyes. The pain in his stomach was terrible.

'Do you understand now, my friend?' said Le Chiffre. 'You will answer my questions. If you don't, you will be badly tortured. Then we will torture the girl. If you still do not speak, we shall kill both of you – painfully.'

Bond opened his eyes.

'Good,' said Le Chiffre, smiling. 'Now, where is the money? You got a cheque for forty million francs. We know that it's somewhere in your room. You went back to your hotel to hide it. When you left to go to the night club, four of my people searched your room. They did not find the cheque. So, where is it?'

Bond stared back at him without speaking.

Le Chiffre moved quickly. He hit Bond across the chest with the stick. Bond closed his eyes against the pain. Then, suddenly, he felt Le Chiffre's burning cigarette against his face. It was a millimetre or two below his left eye.

'Aaaagh!' cried Bond.

'The next time it will be *in* your eye,' said Le Chiffre.

He moved the cigarette away and drank some more coffee.

'You . . . won't be able to cash[37] . . . the cheque,' said Bond. He was breathing heavily. 'The police . . . will know that it's mine.'

Le Chiffre hit Bond across his legs. Bond nearly fainted.

'My friend, I forgot to tell you,' said Le Chiffre. He smiled. 'My story will be that we met again after our game at the Casino. You agreed to have *one more* game. But this time you lost. You were very unhappy and you left Royale to go to . . . well, nobody knows *where* you went. But before you left, you gave me a note. It explains everything. The note means

I'll be able to cash the cheque.' He laughed. 'It's a good story, yes? Now, shall we continue?'

Nobody knows where you went.

'So that was the plan,' thought Bond. He was going to die. There was not enough time for Mathis or Leiter to rescue him.

Then there was Vesper. Soon they would start torturing her too. What would they do to her? He did not want to think about that.

Bond lifted his head. 'No,' he whispered.

Le Chiffre made a small, angry sound. He hit Bond's arms and legs with the stick. Then he pushed the cigarette into Bond's face again. This time it was a millimetre under Bond's right eye.

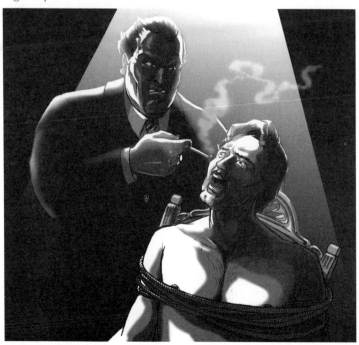

The pain was terrible. Bond's face felt like a ball of fire. He wanted to scream. His eyes filled with tears and he could not see clearly.

'One more chance,' Le Chiffre told him. 'Do you want to be blind, Mr Bond?'

He took the cigarette away again.

'Now,' he began. 'You – '

'Stop,' said a voice, quietly.

There was somebody else in the room.

Bond lifted his head slowly. Le Chiffre was staring at the doorway, behind Bond. He could see the terror in Le Chiffre's eyes.

'SMERSH,' Le Chiffre whispered. 'No! No, I . . .'

'Your two men are dead,' said a voice behind Bond. 'You are a thief and a traitor[38]. I've been sent from Russia to kill you. You're lucky that I only have time to shoot you. I was told to kill you painfully.'

The voice stopped. The room was silent. Somewhere outside a bird began to sing. Bond stared at Le Chiffre's face. It was white with fear.

There was a soft sound – then no other noise at all. Suddenly, a small black hole appeared between Le Chiffre's eyes. A bullet hole. Le Chiffre's head fell to one side and his body hung over the chair.

A hand came from behind Bond. It pulled his head back. Bond looked up into two shining eyes behind a narrow black mask[39]. Above the mask was a hat. Then the hand pushed his head down again.

'You are lucky,' said the voice. 'I have no orders to kill foreign spies. But you're a gambler. One day, perhaps, you will play against one of us. I must let them see that you're a spy.'

The man stood behind Bond's right shoulder. A moment later, he put his hand in front of Bond's face. The hand was holding a long, thin knife. He held it like a pen. He moved the knife above Bond's hand, which was tied to the chair.

He cut four lines into the back of Bond's hand. They looked like the Roman number III with a line underneath. It was the Russian letter sha. It was the first letter of the Russian word *shpion* – spy.

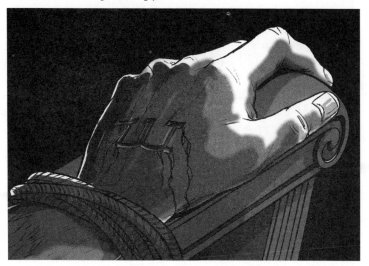

Blood begun to fall on to the floor. Bond had suffered the beatings with the stick and the burning cigarette on his face. But this pain was too much. Everything went black as he fell unconscious.

14

Vesper Explains

James Bond woke up in a bed. He had been dreaming. It had been a bad dream, and he was shaking. Then he heard a woman's voice.

He opened his eyes. Sunlight was shining through the window. He could hear the sound of birds in the garden outside. He turned his head and saw a nurse sitting beside him. She smiled at him.

'Where am I?' he asked.

'You're in a private hospital in Royale,' she said. 'I have come from England to look after you. I'm Nurse Gibson. I'll go and tell the doctor that you're awake. You've been unconscious since they brought you here two days ago. We've been worried.'

Bond closed his eyes for a few minutes. His head and whole body hurt.

The door opened and the doctor came in. Mathis and the nurse followed him. Mathis smiled at Bond, but Bond could see that he was worried.

The doctor was a young Frenchman. He came and stood beside Bond. He spoke clearly in English.

'You have a lot of questions to ask me, Mr Bond,' he said. 'I can tell you most of the answers. Then Monsieur Mathis will speak to you.'

Nurse Gibson gave the doctor a chair to sit in. Then she left the room.

'You have been here about two days,' said the doctor. 'A farmer found your car on his way into Royale. He called the police. Soon, Monsieur Mathis learnt that it was your car. Immediately, he went to Le Chiffre's villa with his men. They found you and Le Chiffre and Miss Lynd. She was not hurt, but she was very shocked. She's much better now. She's staying at Royale. She will stay until you're well enough to go back to England.

'Le Chiffre's two gunmen are dead,' the doctor went on. 'Both men were shot in the back of the head. They were in the same room as Miss Lynd. Le Chiffre was shot between the eyes with the same gun. Did you see him die, Mr Bond?'

'Yes,' said Bond.

'You'll continue to be in pain for several days,' the doctor told him. 'You must rest.' Then he smiled and left the room.

Mathis came and sat in the doctor's chair.

'There's a lot for us to talk about,' he said. 'Our people in Paris and London want to know everything. So does Leiter. Oh, and M spoke to me on the telephone. He's very pleased with you.'

Bond smiled to himself.

'A tall, thin man with one arm came from London,' Mathis went on. 'I think he was Vesper's boss. He spoke with Vesper for a long time. He told her to look after you.'

The man with one arm was Head of S.

'Now,' said Mathis. 'Who killed Le Chiffre?'

'SMERSH,' said Bond.

Mathis looked shocked. 'So they *were* looking for him,' he said. 'What did the killer look like?'

Bond explained everything that had happened. He was very tired when he finished his story.

Mathis put a hand on Bond's shoulder.

'There's one other mystery,' he said. 'Where did you hide the cheque? We've searched your hotel room three times. It isn't there.'

'It *is* there,' Bond said. He laughed. 'Each door has a room number. When Leiter left me that night, I unscrewed the number from the door. I put the folded cheque under it. Then I screwed it back on again. It will still be there.'

After Mathis left, Bond lay back and closed his eyes. He was thinking about Vesper as he fell asleep.

———

Four days later, Bond was feeling much better. He asked to see Vesper. He had been too ill to see her before now. Bond had to ask Vesper some difficult questions. He had to write a report to M. But he didn't want to tell M that Vesper was stupid. She could lose her job.

He expected Vesper to look ill. But she was brown and healthy from the sun. She came into his room smiling.

'I've been to the beach every day,' she explained. 'The doctor said that the sunshine would be good for me. Head of S agreed, and I've found a lovely beach down the coast. I take my lunch and go there each day. I don't come back until the evening.'

Bond could not think of anything to say. He stared at the beautiful girl and felt angry.

'You'll be able to get up soon,' Vesper went on. 'The doctor told me. He said that swimming in the sea will be good for you.'

'It will be weeks before I can swim,' said Bond, angrily. 'But you . . . you go and enjoy yourself!'

'I – I'm sorry,' said Vesper. 'I . . . I wanted to help you.' She began to cry. 'I'm really sorry. This is all my fault.'

Bond put a hand on her arm.

'It's all right, Vesper,' he said gently. 'I'm sorry that I shouted at you. Of course I'll come to the beach with you. It will be wonderful.'

Bond gave her a cigarette.

'What happened after you left me in the night club?' he asked.

'I was stupid,' said Vesper. She looked away from him. 'I couldn't see Mathis, so I went outside. I saw a man waiting in a car. I thought it was Mathis. When I got near, two of Le

Chiffre's men jumped out from behind another car.

'I screamed,' she went on. 'But nobody heard me. The men picked me up and put me in the back of the car. I threw my bag out of the car window. Did it help you?'

'Yes, it did,' said Bond.

But Bond knew that Le Chiffre had wanted him to follow the Citroën.

'I think I fainted,' Vesper went on. 'I don't remember much about the car journey.'

'Did they hurt you after they took you away?' asked Bond.

'No, they tied me to a chair and played cards,' she replied. 'Then they went to sleep. That's how SMERSH got them. My chair was in a corner of the room. I didn't see SMERSH. I heard some strange noises. Then I heard one of the men fall off a chair. After that, the door closed. Then Mathis and the police arrived. That was an hour later. I slept most of the time. Once I heard a terrible scream from very far away.'

'That was probably me,' said Bond.

Vesper started to cry again.

'They did awful things to you, and it's my fault,' she said.

'It's all right,' said Bond. 'It's finished now. Let's forget it.'

'I thought that you'd be angry with me,' said Vesper. 'How can I thank you? Is there something that I can do? I want to do something.' She looked at him and smiled. 'I promise to do *something*.'

Something? He smiled at her.

'You promise?' he said.

She looked into his eyes and put her hand on his hand. 'I promise,' she replied quietly.

After a moment, she picked up her bag and walked to the door.

'Shall I come tomorrow?' she asked.

'Yes, please, Vesper,' said Bond.

15

A Small Hotel

Vesper visited Bond each day. Soon he was well enough to leave the hospital. But he did not want to go to one of the big hotels in Royale.

'I'll find you somewhere outside of the town,' said Vesper.

The next day, she came with his clothes, a hired car and a driver.

'Where are we going?' asked Bond.

'Wait and see,' she said.

Vesper was quiet as they drove along the coast road. Once or twice Bond saw her look into the driver's mirror.

'Is something wrong?' he asked.

'It's nothing,' she said quickly. 'It's silly. I thought that we were being followed.' She looked behind them. 'Oh, look!'

Bond turned and looked through the back window. About half a kilometre away, he saw a black car. It was moving fast.

Bond laughed. 'We can't be the only people using this road,' he said. 'Nobody is following us. We're not doing anything wrong. Stop worrying, Vesper.'

'I expect you're right,' she said. 'And we're nearly there.'

She sat quietly and looked out of the window. But Bond knew that she was nervous. After a few minutes, they came to a small road that went down to the sea.

'Drive down there and stop,' Bond told the driver.

The driver slowed the car and turned off the coast road. He stopped the car behind some trees. Bond and Vesper watched through the back window.

Vesper held Bond's arm tightly. They saw the other car getting closer. It went past and a man's face looked quickly towards them.

Vesper's face was white with fear.

'He looked at us,' she said. 'I *knew* that he was following us.'

'Don't be silly,' said Bond. 'He was looking at that sign.'

Bond pointed to a sign on the corner of the road. The sign read, *Fresh Fruit for Sale*.

'There's probably a fruit farm further down this road,' he said.

'Oh, yes,' said Vesper. 'Of course, you must be right. I'm sorry.'

'Forget it,' said Bond. 'The sun's shining and this is our holiday. The job is finished and there's nothing to worry about. Is there?'

'No, of course there isn't,' said Vesper. She smiled again. 'We're almost there. I hope that you like it.'

After a few minutes they saw the sea. Then a small, brightly-painted hotel appeared between the trees.

'It's not very big,' said Vesper. 'But it's very clean and the food is wonderful.' She looked at Bond. 'Will it be all right?'

'I love it!' he told her.

The car stopped behind the hotel. After a moment, the owner came out to meet them. Monsieur Versoix was about fifty years old.

Versoix took Bond and Vesper to their rooms. Bond's room was on the corner of the building. The window looked out onto the sea. Vesper's room was next door. There was a bathroom between the two rooms. Everything was clean and comfortable.

'Dinner will be at seven-thirty,' Versoix told them. 'I'm sorry we're so quiet. More people will come at the weekend.'

They were speaking outside of Vesper's room. After Versoix left them, Bond pushed Vesper into her room and closed the door. He kissed her gently.

'This is wonderful,' Bond said.

Vesper's eyes were shining and she put her hand on his

arm. They held each other close for a moment. Then Bond kissed her again. He kissed her harder this time, and she fell back on to the bed.

He sat beside her and they looked at each other. Bond put his arm round her. Then she got up and walked over to the window.

'It's going to take some time to get ready for dinner,' Vesper said. 'Go for a swim. I'll unpack your clothes for you.'

Bond came and stood close against her. He put his arms round her.

'Not now,' she said quietly.

Bond kissed her neck.

'All right, Vesper,' he said. He walked over to the door and looked back at her. She had not moved. Then he went out and shut the door.

Bond walked along to his room and sat down on the bed. He could not decide what to do. Have a sleep? Go for a swim? After a moment, he put on his swimming shorts and went downstairs. He went out on to the terrace and down to the beach.

He walked along the edge of the water until he could not see the hotel. Then he went into the sea. It was nearly seven o'clock and the sun was setting. Soon it would disappear.

Bond thought about Vesper as he swam. He knew that he wanted to sleep with her. She was a very secretive person, and there were things that she would never tell him. Bond found this secrecy very exciting.

After some time, Bond came out of the water. He lay on the beach until his body was dry. Then he walked back to the hotel.

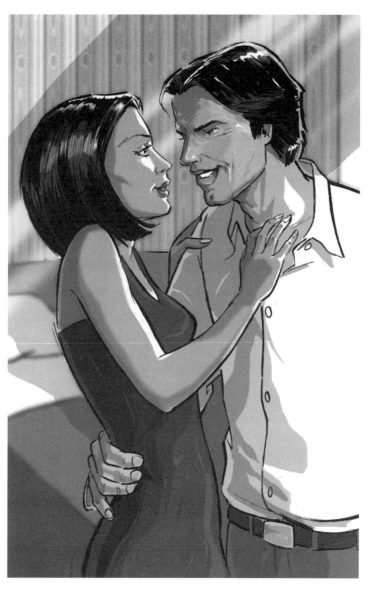

Vesper's eyes were shining and she put her hand on Bond's arm.

16

The Telephone Call

Vesper had unpacked Bond's suitcases and she had put his clothes away. In the bathroom, his toothbrush and shaving things were on a glass shelf. Vesper's toothbrush was next to them. There were also two small bottles. Bond noticed with surprise that one of the bottles contained sleeping pills.

'Perhaps she has problems sleeping,' he thought, 'after what happened to her at Le Chiffre's villa.'

Vesper had run a hot bath for him.

'Thank you, darling!' he called, as he got into the water. 'A bath is exactly what I want now. And then I want you.'

'Well, I want my dinner and some champagne, so hurry!' she called back, laughing.

'All right, all right,' said Bond.

He washed, then got out and dried himself. He dressed in a white shirt and dark blue trousers.

Vesper came into his room without knocking on the door. She was wearing a blue shirt and a dark red skirt. The shirt was the same colour as her eyes.

She held his hand and together they went downstairs.

Their table was on the terrace. They sat down and Bond poured two glasses of champagne. While they ate, Bond told Vesper about his swim. Then they talked about their plans for the following morning. They did not speak about their feelings for each other, but Bond could see the excitement in Vesper's eyes.

They finished the food and opened a second bottle. Then Vesper smiled at him.

'You give me all the things that I like best,' she said. 'I wish that I deserved it.'

60

'What do you mean?' asked Bond, surprised.

Vesper looked at him.

'You really don't know much about me,' she said suddenly. A small shadow seemed to pass between them.

'I know all that I need to know until tomorrow,' said Bond. 'And the next day and the next.' He poured some more champagne. 'You don't know much about me.'

'People are like islands,' said Vesper. 'They can be very close, but they don't really touch.' She laughed suddenly, then she put a hand on his. 'Don't look so worried. My island feels very close to your island tonight.'

The small shadow had passed. They drank their coffee. Then Vesper stood up and put a hand on his shoulder.

'I'm tired,' she said. She kissed him lightly then went into the hotel. A minute or two later, Bond saw the light go on in her room.

He finished his drink. Then he thanked Versoix and his wife for the dinner and went upstairs.

It was only half-past nine when he stepped into Vesper's room. Moonlight shone through the window. Bond closed the door behind him.

He walked across to Vesper's bed.

———

Bond woke up in his own room at dawn. For a time he lay there smiling as he remembered the night before. Then he got out of bed.

Some minutes later, he went quietly out of the hotel and down to the beach. He went into the water and swam.

'I love her,' he said to himself, 'And today I'll ask her to marry me.'

When he got back to the hotel terrace, he was surprised to see Vesper downstairs. She came out of the telephone booth in the lobby. She turned and began to walk quietly up the stairs towards their rooms.

'Vesper,' he called.

Vesper turned quickly and put a hand up to her mouth. She stared at him.

'What's the matter, darling?' he asked.

'N–nothing.' She gave a little laugh. 'You surprised me, that's all. I was just telephoning Mathis.' She spoke quickly. 'I wanted him to get me another dress. I've – I've not got anything nice to wear. Have you been for a swim? Was the water nice?'

'It was wonderful,' said Bond. He was watching her carefully. He knew that she was lying about the telephone call.

'We'll have breakfast on the terrace,' he said. He put his arms round her, but she moved quickly up the stairs.

'It – it was a surprise to see you,' she said. She laughed loudly – too loudly.

Bond wanted to tell her to relax and tell the truth. But instead he smiled.

'I'll see you on the terrace for breakfast,' he said.

Then he went to his room.

17

The Man with the Patch[40]

At breakfast, Bond asked her to tell the truth about the mysterious phone call.

'Why do you ask?' Vesper said angrily. 'Do you think that I've got another lover?' Her eyes filled with tears. 'I've – I've got a very bad headache. I'm going to stay in my room this morning.'

For the next two hours Bond walked along the beach.

When Vesper and Bond met again for lunch, he did not speak about the telephone call. Instead, he talked about his walk that morning. Vesper only said a word or two. She did not look at him.

Then, suddenly, he saw that she was staring past him. Her face was white with fear.

Bond turned his head. A man was sitting at a table on the opposite side of the terrace. The man was about fifty years old with brown hair. He wore a dark suit. Bond guessed that he was a businessman.

'What's the matter, darling?' he asked Vesper.

'It's the man in the car,' she said. 'The man who was following us!'

Bond turned and looked again. Versoix was showing the man the menu. They were talking about the wine. After a moment or two, Versoix walked away.

The man looked at Vesper and Bond for a second. Then he opened a newspaper and began to read. He had a black patch over one eye.

Bond turned to Vesper.

'Are you sure that he's the same man?' he asked.

Her face was still white. She picked up her glass of wine and drank from it. Her hands were shaking.

'I know that he is,' she said. 'My headache is still bad. I'm going to lie down in my room.'

She left the table and walked from the terrace. She didn't look back.

Bond ordered some coffee. Then he got up and walked through the hotel. There was a black Peugeot in the car park. Was it the car that they had seen before? Bond couldn't be sure. He looked inside, but it was empty. The boot was locked. He made a note of the car's number, then he walked back to the terrace. The man was eating and didn't look up. Bond sat in Vesper's chair and watched the other table.

A few minutes later, the man asked for the bill. He paid it and left. Bond heard the Peugeot drive away towards Royale.

Versoix brought Bond his coffee.

'Who was the man at the other table?' Bond asked the hotel owner. 'He looked like a friend of mine.'

'I don't know,' said Versoix. 'I've never seen him before. But he enjoyed his lunch. He said that he would come here again, in a day or two. He comes from Switzerland.'

'Miss Lynd made an early telephone call,' said Bond. 'I must remember to pay for it. A call to Paris. An Elysée number, I think.'

Mathis had an Elysée telephone number, Bond remembered.

'Thank you, Monsieur, but there's nothing to pay,' said Versoix. 'There was no reply to Miss Lynd's call to Paris. But it was an Invalides number, not an Elysée number.'

18

Gettler

Two days later, a taxi came to take Vesper to Royale. She told Bond that she needed some medicine.

That night, Vesper tried to be cheerful. She drank a lot of champagne. When they went upstairs, she took him into her bedroom. They made love, but afterwards she cried into her pillow. Bond went to his room feeling very unhappy.

He could not sleep. Early in the morning he heard a door open softly. Some small sounds came from downstairs. Bond was sure that Vesper was in the telephone booth. Very soon after, he heard her door close softly.

This was Saturday. On Sunday, the man with the black patch came back again. Bond had telephoned Mathis and asked him to check the number of the Peugeot. Mathis had telephoned back a little later.

'The car was hired two weeks ago,' Mathis had told Bond. 'The man's name is Adolph Gettler, and he comes from Switzerland. Gettler gave the car-hire company the address of a bank in Zurich.'

'Did you contact the Swiss police?' asked Bond.

'Of course,' said Mathis. 'The bank does have an account in Gettler's name. He doesn't use it very often. They believe that Gettler's business is clocks and watches.'

Bond had told this to Vesper. Now the man with the patch had appeared again. Vesper quickly got up from the table and went to her room.

Bond finished his lunch then followed her. Her door was locked, but she opened it for him. Bond took her across to the bed and they sat down.

'Vesper, we can't continue like this,' Bond said. 'You must tell me what all this is about, or we must leave now.'

She said nothing.

'My darling,' he said. 'That first morning, I wanted to ask you to marry me. Please tell me what's wrong. Then, perhaps, we can go back and – '

'You would have married me?' she said.

She began to cry. Then she pulled him close.

'Tell me,' he said. 'Tell me what's hurting you.'

Vesper held his face in her hands and kissed him.

'Leave me for a little while,' she said. 'Let me think. I'm trying to do what is best. Please believe me.'

She took him to the door and they kissed again. Then Bond went out and she shut the door behind him.

That night at dinner she seemed happy and excited. They sat and finished the bottle of champagne. Then they went up to her room. They made love for two hours.

'You must go now,' said Vesper, after Bond had slept for a short time in her arms.

He kissed her eyes and her mouth.

'Look at me,' she said. 'And let me look at you.'

She looked at every line of his face. Her eyes were full of tears as she kissed him gently.

'Goodnight, my dearest love,' she said.

He went to the door and looked back.

'Sleep well, my darling,' he said. 'Don't worry, everything is all right now.'

He closed the door softly and walked back to his room.

19

The Letter

Versoix brought him the letter in the morning. He ran into Bond's room holding the envelope.

'There has been a terrible accident,' he said. 'Madame ...'

Bond jumped out of bed and ran to her door. It was open and sunlight lit up the room. Vesper was lying on the bed. Bond could see only her black hair above the sheet.

He fell down on to his knees beside the bed and pulled back the sheet. She was asleep, he told himself. She must be. Her eyes were closed.

But she was not breathing.

Versoix touched Bond's shoulder. He pointed to the sleeping pills bottle on the floor beside the bed. The bottle was empty.

Bond stood up and took the letter from Versoix. He walked back to his room and sat on the bed. He looked out of the window at the sea for a moment or two. Then he opened the envelope.

It was not a long letter. After the first few words, he read it quickly.

My darling James

I love you with all my heart, and I hope that you still love me. This will be the last moment that you will love me. So, goodbye my darling, while we still love each other.

I am a double agent[41] for the Russians. I became an agent for them a year after the war. I have worked for them since then. I was in love with a Polish man who was in the British Royal Air Force. After the war, he worked for M. M sent him

68

It was not a long letter. After the first few words, Bond read it quickly.

back to Poland, but the Russians caught him and tortured him. He told them about me. They found me and forced me to work for them. They said that they would kill my lover if I didn't work for them.

I had to tell them about you. I told them that you had a job to do at Royale. They put the microphones in your room. They knew that your job was something to do with Le Chiffre.

They didn't hurt me at the villa because I worked for the Russians. Then I discovered what Le Chiffre did to you. I had begun to fall in love with you. They wanted me to find out things from you when you were in hospital. I refused. I knew that they would kill my lover in Poland.

Then I saw the man with the black patch in the hotel. I hoped that I could escape from them, but they followed us. You can't get away from SMERSH.

I didn't tell you because it would be the end of our love. There were only two things that I could do. I could wait to be killed by SMERSH, but then they would kill you, too. Or I could kill myself.

That is all, my darling love. I can't tell you much that will help you. The Paris number was Invalides 55200. I never met any of them in London. Messages came to me through a shop at 450 Charing Cross Place.

It's late now and I'm tired.

My love, my love

V.

Bond threw the letter down. He stood up and looked out of the window at the sea. A moment later, he dressed and went downstairs to the telephone booth.

He telephoned London. While he waited, he thought about Vesper. A spy. A double agent. He thought about all the agents that she had put in danger. All the secrets that she had given to the Russians.

Suddenly, he heard a voice at the other end of the telephone.

'This is 007 speaking,' said Bond. 'Pass on[42] this message immediately. 3030 was a double agent. What? Yes, I said "was". The bitch[43] is dead now.'

Points for Understanding

1

1 Which country did Le Chiffre work for?
2 Why did Le Chiffre have to win at Royale?
3 Why did Bond have to beat Le Chiffre at baccarat?
4 Was Bond going to work alone at Royale?

2

1 Why did Mathis play the radio so loudly in Bond's room?
2 What did Mathis tell Bond about his new assistant?
3 Bond had a problem with his new assistant. What was it?

3

1 The girl and Bond had thoughts about each other. What were these thoughts?
2 What happened after Bond left the bar?

4

Three people were killed in the explosion. Is this true or false?

5

1 Complete these sentences:
   a   Felix Leiter worked for ....
   b   Bond warned Leiter about ....
   c   Bond took a .... and a .... from the drawer.
   d   The French group had planned to kill ....
      people.

2 Bond explained the game of baccarat to Vesper.
  Are these facts true or false?
  a   The banker bets first.
  b   Only four people can play.
  c   Everyone is given two cards.
  d   If a player has a four and a five, he wins.
  e   A player has a King and an ace. If he takes a third card – a
      nine – he wins.
  f   The banker and Bond look at their cards at the same time.

6

Who played against Le Chiffre first, the Greek or Bond?

7

Complete this sentence.
Bond won the first bet, but by the end of the chapter he
....

8

1 How did Felix Leiter help Bond?
2 Le Chiffre needed fifty million francs. Why did he bet again?
3 What happened when Bond accepted the bet and what was he
  told to do?
4 Why did Bond tell the waiter to give the 'walking stick' to
  Leiter?

9

1 This chapter is called 'Winner and Loser'. Who won and who
  lost?
2 Why did the game end when Le Chiffre left the table?

10

1 Where did Bond meet Vesper?
2 'Something was wrong'. Why did Bond think this?
3 What did Bond decide to do?

11

1 Who was driving the Citroën and who else was in it?
2 Who was driving the Bentley?

12

1 'Bond could not control the heavy car'. Why not?
2 What happened to Bond and his car?
3 Where did Le Chiffre take Bond and Vesper?

13

1 Why did Le Chiffre torture Bond?
2 What did Le Chiffre plan to tell the police about Bond?
3 Bond thought that he was going to die, but he didn't. Why not?
4 What did the man from SMERSH do to Bond?

14

1 Was Bond in France or England when he woke up?
2 Who had found Bond and Vesper?
3 Where had Bond hidden the cheque?
4 Why did Vesper cry when she visited Bond?

15

1 Why was Vesper nervous?
2 What did Bond find exciting about Vesper?

16

1 'People are like islands,' said Vesper. What did she mean?
2 The next morning, Bond decided to ask Vesper ....

17

1 At breakfast, Vesper was angry. At lunch, she was frightened. Why?
2 Bond learnt that Vesper had lied about the telephone call to Paris. How?

18

1 The man with the black patch was called ....
2 He had hired ....

19

1 'There has been a terrible accident,' Versoix said. (page 68)
   What had happened?
2 'There were only two things that I could do.' Vesper wrote in her letter.
   What were these things and which one did she choose?
3 'The bitch is dead now.' (page 71)
   Why did Bond say this about Vesper?

Glossary

1 **memorandum** (page 9)
   a short written statement with information about a subject. It is passed between people in a government, organization, or business.
2 **treasurer** (page 9)
   someone who controls the money that belongs to an organization.
3 **trade union** (page 9)
   an organization of workers. A trade union tries to improve pay and conditions at work. Trade unions are often simply called unions.
4 **financial ruin** (page 9)
   the loss of all your money.
5 **francs** (page 9)
   money used in the past in France, Belgium and some other countries. *Francs* have now been replaced with *Euros*.
6 **investment** – *to invest* (page 9)
   something that you spend money on now because it will bring you more money in the future.
7 **baccarat** (page 9)
   a game played, especially in casinos, using *playing cards*. Playing cards are pieces of strong card or paper with numbers and pictures printed on them. There are four *suits* – or different families – in a *pack* (or *deck*) of playing cards. These are *spades*, *hearts*, *diamonds* and *clubs*.

 SPADES   HEARTS  DIAMONDS   CLUBS

Each suit has 13 cards in it: Ace, 2, 3, 4, 5, 6, 7, 8, 9, 10, Jack, Queen and King.
The *banker* is the person who keeps the money while the game is being played. The *croupier* is the person in control of the game. The croupier's job is to give and collect the cards. The cards are taken from the *shoe*. The player *turns over* the cards, so that they are *face-up* and the numbers and pictures can be seen. After he has looked at the cards, he turns them *face-down*, so that the numbers and pictures are towards the table and cannot be seen.

In baccarat, two cards each are given to the banker and to the player. If the two cards *add up* to an amount, together they *total* that amount. The player whose cards add up to nine or the total closest to nine is the winner. If the cards add up to less than nine, the player can ask for a third card. If the cards add up to more than nine, the player loses. When you *bet*, you risk an amount of money by saying what you think will happen, especially in a race or game. You lose the money if you are wrong and win more if you are right. In baccarat the players bet that their cards' total will be closest to nine. The players bet with *plaques*, which are small, round coloured objects that you use instead of money in a gambling game.

8 **gambler** – *to gamble* (page 9)

if you play a game to win money you are gambling. A person who gambles is a *gambler*.

9 **CIA** (page 11)

the *Central Intelligence Agency*: a US government organization that collects secret political, military and other information about other countries. The CIA also protects secret information about the US.

10 **microphone** (page 13)

a piece of equipment used for making someone's voice louder.

11 **winnings** (page 13)

money that you win when you are gambling.

12 **cashier** (page 13)

someone whose job is to receive or give money in a shop, bank, casino, etc.

13 **concierge** (page 13)

someone whose job is to help people staying in a hotel. A *concierge* deals with people's problems and gives them information.

14 **cable** (page 13)

a message that you send by *telegraph*. A *cable* was used in the past for short, important messages.

15 **code** (page 13)

a system of words, numbers, or signs used for sending secret messages.

16 **cover** (page 13)

a false story that is used for hiding who someone really is.

17 **monsieur** (page 14)

the word used as a title for a man, like 'Mr', in French-speaking countries.

18 **chimney** (page 14)
a tube or passage that takes smoke from a fire up through a building and out through the roof.

19 **explosion** – *to explode* (page 18)
when something bursts with a lot of force and a loud noise, it *explodes*. An *explosion* is an occasion when something explodes. An object that can cause an explosion is called an *explosive*.

20 **shattered** – *to shatter* (page 18)
to break suddenly into a lot of small pieces.

21 **holster** (page 22)
a leather container for a gun, that is fixed to a belt or worn over your shoulder.

22 **walking stick** (page 29)
a long strong piece of wood, usually with a handle at the top. You use a *walking stick* to help you walk.

23 **passed** – *to pass* (page 29)
to decide not to play a card or make a bet in a card game.

24 **fainted** – *to faint* (page 32)
to become unconscious for a short time.

25 **bullet** (page 36)
a small piece of metal that is shot from a gun. A bullet causes serious damage to the person or thing it hits.

26 **fingerprints** (page 36)
a mark that you leave on something when you touch it. The mark shows the pattern of lines on the skin of your fingers.

27 **screwdriver** (page 38)
a screw is a thin, pointed piece of metal used for joining one thing to another. A screwdriver is a tool used for turning screws.

28 **Bentley** (page 41)
a large, expensive and comfortable car of very high quality.

29 **handle** (page 41)
the part of an object that you hold in your hand when you use it.

30 **sack** (page 41)
a large, strong bag for storing and carrying things.

31 **crossroads** (page 41)
a place where one road crosses another.

32 **boot** (page 42)
the covered space at the back of a car, used for carrying bags and other things.

33 **spikes** (page 43)
something sharp and pointed, especially a piece of metal or wood.
34 **conscious** (page 43)
awake and able to see, hear, and think. The opposite is *unconscious*.
35 **torture** (page 47)
extreme pain caused by someone or something, especially as a
punishment or to make someone say something.
36 **naked** (page 47)
not wearing any clothes. The opposite is *dressed*.
37 **cash** – *to cash a cheque* (page 48)
to exchange a cheque for its value in notes and coins.
38 **traitor** (page 50)
someone who tells secrets about their own country to a country
that is their enemy.
39 **mask** (page 50)
something you wear to cover part or all of your face. You can use it
to hide who you are, or for decoration.
40 **patch** (page 63)
a piece of cloth, plastic, etc. used for covering one eye. An *eye
patch*.
41 **double agent** (page 68)
someone who finds out secret information for a government but
also for that government's enemy.
42 **pass on** – to pass on something (page 71)
to give someone something that someone else has given you,
especially information.
43 **bitch** (page 71)
an bad word used for a woman. A *bitch* is also a female dog.

*Dictionary extracts adapted from the Macmillan English Dictionary © Bloomsbury Publishing Plc 2002
and © A & C Black Publishers Ltd 2005.*

Exercises

Vocabulary: words from the story

Complete the sentences with the correct words from the box.
There are four extra words.

> repayment   armed   destruction   chief   spies   gambler
> worthless   treasurer   assistant   agent   memorandum
> financial   investment

1   Le Chiffre controlled the trade union's money. Le Chiffre was
    the union's ....

2   The Head of Section S sent a written statement to M. S sent M a
    ....

3   James Bond worked for the British Secret Intelligence Service.
    Bond was an intelligence ....

4   The Russian words *smyert shpionam* mean DEATH TO
    ....

5   Le Chiffre liked to play cards for money in casinos. He was a
    ....

6   His guards always carried guns. They were always
    ....

7   Le Chiffre's girlfriend told us about his money problems. She
    said that he was close to .... ruin.

8   She told us that Le Chiffre's investments had lost all their value.
    They are now completely ....

9   M sent someone to help Bond. He sent him an
    ....

Vocabulary: meanings of words from the story

Put the words and phrases in the box next to the correct meanings.

> section   handsome   francs   dangerous   chief   argue
> information   cashier   baccarat   reply   expert   be silent
> contact   explode   gamble   make trouble   personal assistant
> safety   arrange to meet   add up

1	French money (in 1950)	
2	not safe	
3	get in touch with	
4	disagree	
5	a person who works at a cash desk	
6	answer	
7	someone who knows a lot about something	
8	say nothing	
9	good-looking	
10	go off (of bombs) / blow up	
11	play cards for money	
12	cause problems	
13	agree to see each other	
14	private helper	
15	total (verb)	
16	main / most important	
17	security	
18	department	
19	intelligence	
20	the name of a card game played in casinos	

Writing: rewrite sentences

Rewrite the sentences using the words and phrases in the previous exercise to replace the underlined words.

> **Example**   Le Chiffre <u>works for</u> Russian Intelligence.
> You write: *Le Chiffre is a Russian Intelligence agent.*

1 How much is that in <u>French money</u>?

_____

2 Bond did not <u>argue</u> with M.

_____

3 The girl <u>said nothing</u>.

_____

4 Bond was <u>good-looking</u>.

_____

5 Le Chiffre <u>played cards for money</u>.

_____

6 His guards won't <u>cause problems</u>.

_____

7 Bond <u>agreed to see</u> Leiter in the hotel lobby.

_____

8 The cable did not need <u>an answer</u>.

_____

9 A bomb <u>went off</u> outside the bar.

_____

10 Mathis <u>got in touch with</u> Paris.

_____

Story Outline: complete part of the story

Complete the text with the words from the box.

> Bond Bulgarian told man them filled hotel first contained
> bar promised two was other explosion smoke case bomb
> pressed throw blue expected killed waited protected

There were three [1].. agents. One of
[2]........................ waited outside the [3]............................... .
Two of them [4]....................................... near the Hermitage
[5]........................ . Their orders were to kill James Bond.
The [6]........................ men had cases. One case [7]........................
red and the [8]....................................... was blue. They had been
[9]........................ that the blue [10]........................ contained a
smoke [11]........................ . The red case [12]...................................
explosives. One man had to [13]............................... the explosives
at [14]................................... . Then the other [15]........................
had to press a switch on the [16]................................. case to
make a lot of smoke. They [17].. to
escape through the [18].................................... . But each camera
case was [19]....................................... with explosives. The
men had been tricked. One man [20]..
the switch on the blue case [21].. .
It exploded and [22].. them both.
They had been [23].. two million
francs for killing Bond. Bond was not hurt because a tree
[24].. him from the
[25]................................. .

Vocabulary Focus: *both*

The word *both* always means two things or two people. Put the word in the correct place in the sentences.

1   The red case and the blue case contained explosives.

     ....

2   The tall man and the thin man were Bulgarian.

     ....

3   We liked the two pictures so much that we decided to buy them.

     ....

4   The man and the woman were seen at the hotel and then later on at the casino.

     ....

Grammar Focus: the past perfect tense

There are several events in the story where one event happened before another. In this case, the past perfect is used to describe the event that happened first.

Earlier that afternoon, Bond had asked his headquarters in London for more money.

Join the sentences by using words like *when* and *already* and putting the verb in the past perfect.

> **Example**   Bond was at the hotel. Le Chiffre was in town already.
> You write: *When Bond arrived at his hotel, Le Chiffre had already arrived in town.*

1   Bond went to bed at 3 a.m. He checked his messages first.

2   Bond entered the bar. The American was already there.

84

3 The Greek lost two games. Bond joined the table.

---

4 The gunman threatened Bond. Bond placed a bet.

---

5 The men took Vesper. Bond hid the cheque.

Vocabulary: anagrams

The letters of each word are mixed up. Write the words correctly. The first one is an example.

Example GINTENIECELL   the 'I' of CIA
         INTELLIGENCE

1	FAILINANC	an adjective meaning money; there is a London newspaper for business people called the FT or .... Times
2	ECONCIRGE	a French word: a person whose job is to help guests in big hotels; he or she works at or near the front desk
3	TRUEROT	to cause extreme pain to someone in order to make them give information
4	SUNSCICONOU	Bond was injured in the car crash; he hit his head and was not awake for a time; he was ...
5	DANEK	wearing no clothes
6	KIPES	something sharp, pointed and made of metal

7	RIVERDCREWS	a tool for turning screws
8	PINGERRFINT	a mark left by fingers and hands which the police can use to identify criminals
9	BUTLLE	a small piece of shaped metal that is fired from a gun
10	SHORTLE	a holder for a gun – worn under the arm or at the waist
11	LABEC	an old word for a telegram; a length of wire
12	TINMENVEST	money that is put into a business in order to earn more money in the future
13	LOSEXPION	the result of a bomb going off
14	YIMNECH	a tube or passage that takes smoke away from a fire and out of a building
15	MUDORMEMAN	a written document in a government organization or a business office
16	RAGBLEM	a person who risks money in a casino
17	RESTATH	to break into small pieces – especially used with glass
18	RATIORT	someone who sells secrets to another country
19	SKAM	this is used to cover your face so that people do not recognize you, or it is worn to protect your face
20	CHIBT	a bad word for a woman; a female dog

Vocabulary Choice: words which are related in meaning

Which word is most closely related? Look at the example and circle the word most closely related to the word in bold.

Example: **chief**   post   (main)   target   agent

1	**ruin**	building	border	ancient	destruction
2	**funds**	enjoyment	money	bases	titles
3	**intelligence**	information	politeness	brightness	examination
4	**villa**	football	town	country	house
5	**armed**	disabled	weapons	feet	peaceful
6	**secret**	office	public	occupation	private
7	**extra**	usual	common	additional	nearer
8	**expert**	experienced	import	radio	business
9	**strange**	familiar	common	normal	unusual
10	**enemy**	opponent	assistant	support	medicine
11	**stare**	steps	look	hear	feel
12	**difficult**	easy	soft	choice	hard
13	**nervous**	uneasy	happy	comfortable	safe
14	**softly**	quietly	barely	scarcely	hardly

Published by Macmillan Heinemann ELT
Between Towns Road, Oxford OX4 3PP
Macmillan Heinemann ELT is an imprint of
Macmillan Publishers Limited
Companies and representatives throughout the world
Heinemann is a registered trademark of Pearson Education, used under licence

ISBN 978 0 2300 3749 6
ISBN 978 1 4050 8744 5 (with CD pack)

Casino Royale by Ian Fleming. Copyright © Ian Fleming
Publications Ltd, 1953.
*Ian Fleming asserts his rights to be identified as the author of the original work
of which this Graded Reader is an adaptation.*

This retold version by John Escott for Macmillan Readers
First published 2006
Text © Macmillan Publishers Limited 2006
Design and illustration © Macmillan Publishers Limited 2006

This version first published 2006

Illustrated by Pete Smith
Cover photograph by Corbis

Printed in Thailand
2012 2011 2010
8 7 6 5 4

with CD pack
2012 2011 2010
10 9 8 7